Donated to St. Helena's Children Library
by poet's
First & Second Grades
Peace First ♡

kindness

inclusion

forgiveness

acceptance

true friend

communication

empathy

THE
FRUIT SALAD
FRIEND

Recipe for a
TRUE FRIEND

by Maria Dismondy art by Kathryn Selbert

Copyright 2017 Maria Cini Dismondy
Illustrations by Kathryn Selbert
Book Design by Emily O'Malley

First Printing 2018
All rights reserved.
Printed in China
Chloe is a great friend but quickly learns not
everyone at school can say the same thing.
By listening to her heart and staying true to
herself, Chloe learns the values, traits and
characteristics that truly matter when it
comes to cooking up lasting friendships.

Dismondy, Maria Cini (1978-)
The Fruit Salad Friend: Recipe for a True Friend
1. Acts of Kindness 2. Empathy 3. Family Life
4. Fiction 5. Relationships

ISBN: 978-0-9976085-2-6
LCCN: 2017945515

Cardinal Rule Press
5449 Sylvia
Dearborn Heights, MI 48125
www.cardinalrulepress.com

BEFORE READING:

* Read the title of the book.
Ask your child if they know what a recipe is.
Talk about the vocabulary word "ingredients" too.

* This book is about a friend. Name a friend of yours.
Why are they your friend?

DURING READING:

* Ask your child to point out what happens when
Chloe gets upset (example: her face feels hot).
What does she do to calm herself down?

* Discuss the word "empathy." Pick out one of
the friendship situations and ask your child to put
themselves in the shoes of Chloe. How would they feel?

AFTER READING:

* Read the recipe at the back of the book. Tell your child what
you consider to be a key ingredient to a true friend.

* Pick out a recipe and cook a treat together.

* Help your child by role playing tricky friendship conversations.
Encouraging your child to spend time with those who
treat them kindly and accept them for who they are
is really important.

'For my mom, with love'
K.S.

To my friends, old and new:
You mean the world to me!
M.D.

Chloe loved playing outside. She loved fruit--eating it and growing it in the garden with her Papa. But most of all, she loved school.

It was the first thing she thought about when she woke up, and it was the last thing she thought about before going to bed.

But this year, something was different at school. Chloe just couldn't put her finger on exactly what was different.

Chloe hurried onto the bus. She was excited to read the note Papa left in her lunchbox. She couldn't resist sneaking a peek before lunch. But her smile quickly faded and tears filled her eyes.

"This is going to be the BEST birthday party EVER...IF you were lucky enough to get invited..." announced the girl across the seat. All the other girls around Chloe on the bus held pink envelopes.

"That's okay. I didn't get an invitation either," whispered the girl, Margaret, sitting behind her.

Chloe took a deep breath
and focused on finishing
her apple.

A few days later on the playground, Chloe felt her lip trembling.

"We can't play with you today. Sorry! Maybe tomorrow," snarled one of the boys.

"Why not?" Chloe managed to ask.

"Because we said so!" one of the boys replied.

"You're in a bad mood. I'll play with someone else," Chloe said courageously before they walked away from her, laughing. Chloe started to hum one of her favorite songs as she walked toward another group of kids. Her lip stopped trembling and she enjoyed the rest of recess.

The bell rang for lunch. The first thing Chloe
noticed at the table was her face getting hot. She
knew why--the lunchroom drama was building.

"Jenny is my best friend now. Go sit somewhere else," said Chloe's usual lunch buddy.

Chloe stood up. "Fine. I will sit by someone who is nice to me." Chloe found another seat and slowly counted to ten to fast forward what just happened. She felt the heat leaving her face now.

Back at home, Chloe sat at the kitchen table as Papa talked about his day. As she stared at the fruit bowl, something clicked. Chloe realized that while all fruits are good, you only put the sweet ones in a fruit salad. In her heart, she knew which friends had been sweet and which were a little sour.

"Is everything okay, Chloe?" asked Papa.

"Yes, I think so. I've had a problem but I think I've figured out a way to solve it."

Chloe couldn't wait for school the next day. She felt like a chef with a new recipe. A doctor with a cure. A superhero ready to save the day!

The next afternoon, Chloe's cheeks tingled from smiling so much. She headed right over to Margaret, who was sitting alone on the bench. She sat down and Margaret smiled. They giggled when they noticed they each had fruit salad snacks!

Something was different at school.
Something had indeed changed.

Chloe loved playing outside. She loved fruit and she loved school. Above all, Chloe loved being a good friend and looking for the sweetness in others, too.

RECIPE FOR FRIENDSHIP

Ingredients:

2 Tbsp. Kindness
½ Cup Inclusion
2 Cups Acceptance

3 tsp. Empathy
3 Cups Communication
3 Tbsp. Forgiveness

Directions:

Friendship begins with a big dollop of **kindness** - always treat others the way you wish to be treated. Next, add a serving of **inclusion** and remember there's always room for more friends. Combine this with **acceptance** and embrace everyone's unique qualities.

Mix in **empathy** by imagining how others might feel and stir in **communication** by speaking up when you need to express an emotion. Last but not least, clean up by asking for **forgiveness** and forgiving your friends, too. Sprinkle with fun, laughter and silliness. Bake for 365 days.

Yields:

Endless friendships!

10 TIPS TO BOOST YOUR CHILD'S FRIENDSHIP MAKING SKILLS

Friends play an enormous part in our kids' lives. The good news is that making friends involves skills which can be learned. Here are ways you can make a difference in your child's social life.

1. **Reinforce smiling!** A trait that well-liked kids use often is to smile, so reinforce your child's smiling efforts. "What a great smile!" or "That smile of yours always wins people over."

2. **Boost manners.** When it comes to friends, manners *do* count and are appreciated by other parents.

3. **Encourage listening.** Listening lets a friend know another is concerned about their needs. Tell your child, "Focus on what your friend is saying. Hear their words!"

4. **Teach deal breakers.** Learning Rock, Paper, Scissors, flipping a coin, and "Eeny, Meeny, Miny, Moe" are great for reducing conflicts, breaking ties, and deciding who goes first.

5. **Stress assertiveness.** Encouraging kids to "look at the color of the speaker's eyes" helps them appear more confident as well as interested in the speaker's words.

6. **Make time for play.** Carve time into your child's schedule for play dates and social interactions to expand social competence.

7. **Practice introductions.** "Hi! My name is John." "Glad to meet you." "You're good at soccer." "Do you live around here?" "Do you go to school here?"

8. **Teach kindness.** Popular kids care, share, and are helpful. Praise your child's prosocial behaviors so she knows kindness matters.

9. **Talk about emotions.** Kids can't care about others if they can't recognize feelings. So, use emotions and words, and point out facial expressions, voice, tone, and body language.

10. **Teach friendship skills.** Friendship is comprised of skills like taking turns, having a conversation, joining a group, problem solving and listening. Choose one skill, explain the value, show how to use it and practice it until your child can use it alone. Add a new skill when that one is mastered.

Dr. Michele Borba, is an educational psychologist, speaker, parenting expert and bestselling author of 24 books. Her latest book is *UnSelfie: Why Empathetic Kids Succeed in Our All-About-Me World.* For more information: micheleborba.com and Twitter: @micheleborba.

When Maria was a little girl she was teased for her curly hair and favorite lunchbox fare, spaghetti in a hot dog bun. Many moons later, these and other real-life moments continue to fuel what is now her critically acclaimed children's book writing career. Maria has penned nine books that feature stories with topics ranging from anti-bullying to overcoming adversity, to friendship trials and tribulations, and beyond. Maria is dedicated to empowering those around her through her roles as author, teacher, public speaker, community leader and friend. Maria is intentional about making each day count and lives in southeast Michigan with her high school sweetheart husband, three kids and two pet snails.

Kathryn Selbert is a freelance illustrator currently living in New Haven, Connecticut, with her French bulldog Margot. She earned her BFA in Illustration from the Rhode Island School of Design (RISD). Her work is inspired by the people she meets in her everyday life, our colorful world, flora and fauna, and having fun.

kindness

inclusion

forgiveness

acceptance

true friend

communication

empathy